I Can Be Anything!
I CAN BE A SCIENTIST

By Michou Franco

Please visit our website, www.garethstevens.com. For a free color catalog of all our high-quality books, call toll free 1-800-542-2595 or fax 1-877-542-2596.

Cataloging-in-Publication Data

Names: Franco, Michou.
Title: I can be a scientist / Michou Franco.
Description: New York : Gareth Stevens Publishing, 2018. | Series: I can be anything! | Includes index.
Identifiers: ISBN 9781482463293 (pbk.) | ISBN 9781482463316 (library bound) | ISBN 9781482463309 (6 pack)
Subjects: LCSH: Science–Vocational guidance–Juvenile literature. | Scientists–Juvenile literature.
Classification: LCC Q147.F73 2018 | DDC 502.3–dc23

First Edition

Published in 2018 by
Gareth Stevens Publishing
111 East 14th Street, Suite 349
New York, NY 10003

Copyright © 2018 Gareth Stevens Publishing

Editor: Therese Shea
Designer: Sarah Liddell

Photo credits: Cover, p. 1 (kid) India Picture/Shutterstock.com; cover, p. 1 (background) Timof/Shutterstock.com; p. 5 Pressmaster/Shutterstock.com; p. 7 wavebreakmedia/Shutterstock.com; p. 9 Mediaphotos/Shutterstock.com; pp. 11, 24 (hammer) Alfafoto/Shutterstock.com; pp. 13, 24 (planet) pkproject/Shutterstock.com; p. 15 Alexandra_F/Shutterstock.com; p. 17 Joe Raedle/Staff/Getty Images News/Getty Images; p. 19 Minerva Studio/Shutterstock.com; pp. 21, 24 (medicine) funnyangel/Shutterstock.com; p. 23 goodmoments/Shutterstock.com.

All rights reserved. No part of this book may be reproduced in any form without permission in writing from the publisher, except by a reviewer.

Printed in the United States of America

CPSIA compliance information: Batch #CS17GS: For further information contact Gareth Stevens, New York, New York at 1-800-542-2595.

Contents

Looking for Answers..... 4

Kinds of Scientists........ 8

Hello, Mr. Fox!......... 18

Let's Be Scientists!...... 22

Words to Know 24

Index................. 24

Scientists ask questions.
They look for answers.

Scientists find out how things work!

Some study plants. They help farmers grow our food!

Some study rocks.
They use tools
like hammers!

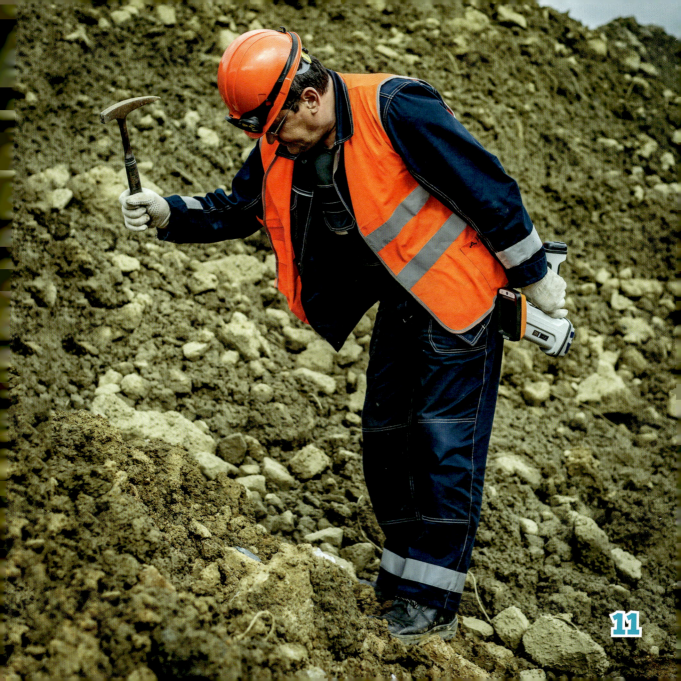

Some study planets and stars.
Our sun is a star!

Some study bugs.
They find new kinds
of bugs!

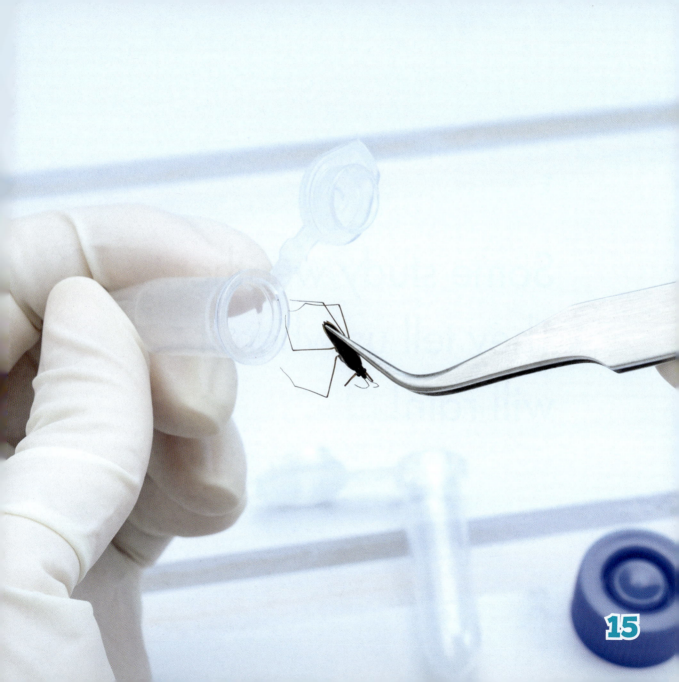

Some study weather. They tell us when it will rain!

This is Mr. Fox.
He is a scientist.

Mr. Fox works in a lab.
He makes medicine
that helps sick people.

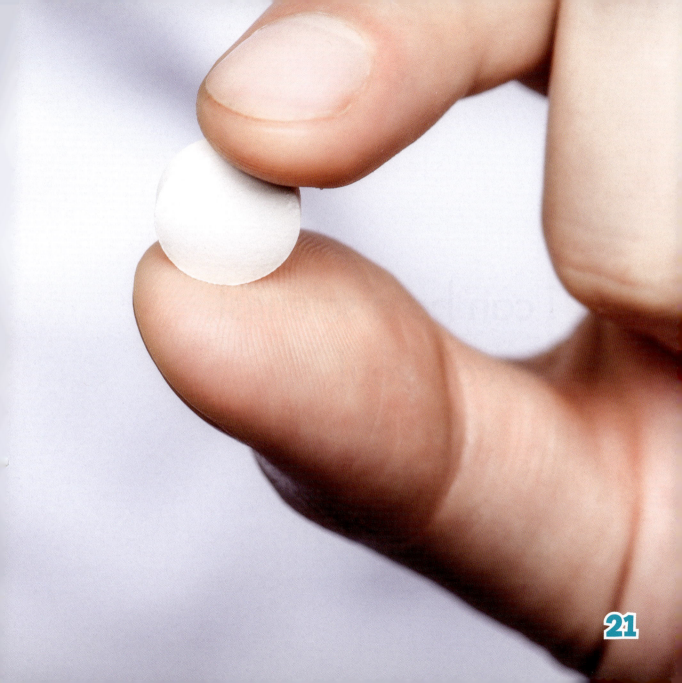

I can be a scientist.
So can you!

Words to Know

hammer   medicine   planet

Index

bugs 14
medicine 20
planets 12

plants 8
stars 12
weather 16